RUFUS

SIMON BARTRAM

templar
books

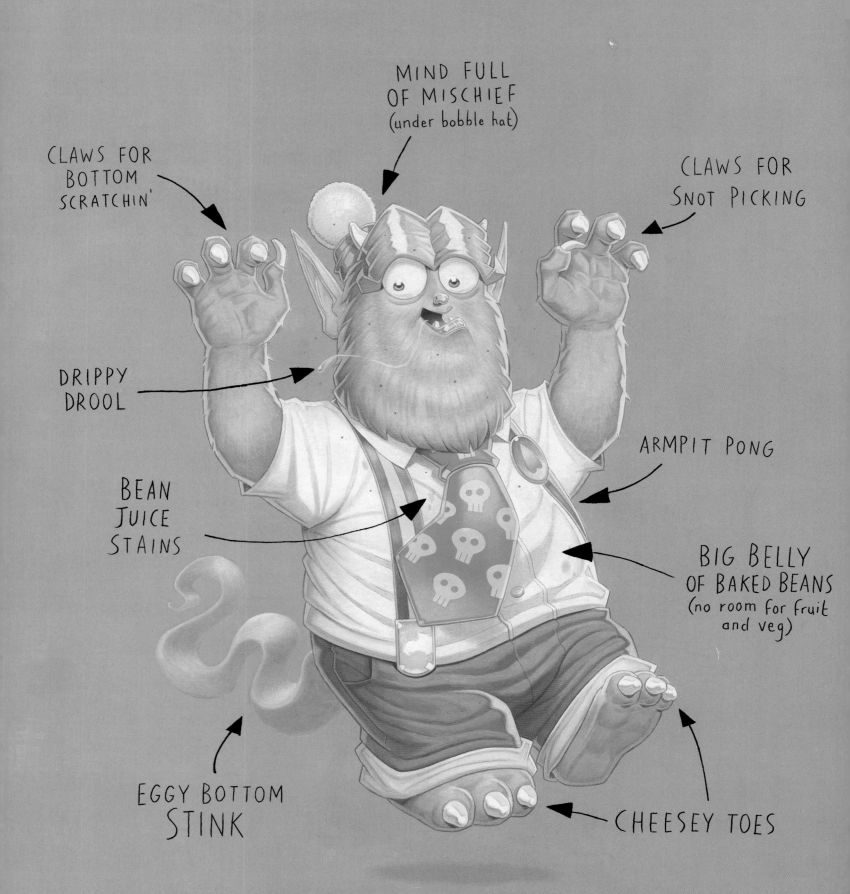

MIND FULL
OF MISCHIEF
(under bobble hat)

CLAWS FOR
BOTTOM
SCRATCHIN'

CLAWS FOR
SNOT PICKING

DRIPPY
DROOL

ARMPIT PONG

BEAN
JUICE
STAINS

BIG BELLY
OF BAKED BEANS
(no room for fruit
and veg)

EGGY BOTTOM
STINK

CHEESEY TOES

From his big sharp teeth to his super-stinky bottom,
RUFUS was a truly splendid monster.

Unfortunately, though, he didn't feel like a
TIP-TOP SCARY MONSTER.

And he didn't feel like a **TIP-TOP SCARY MONSTER**
for one VERY important reason . . .

Rufus had nobody to frighten!

Most days, Rufus would **roar** at the rocks,

rage at the clouds and **rant** at the sun.

Somehow, though, it just didn't feel right.

What he really needed to **roar** and **rage**
and **rant** at, he thought, was a

PEOPLEY PERSON!

Rufus had read about Peopley Persons in books
written by terribly important experts.

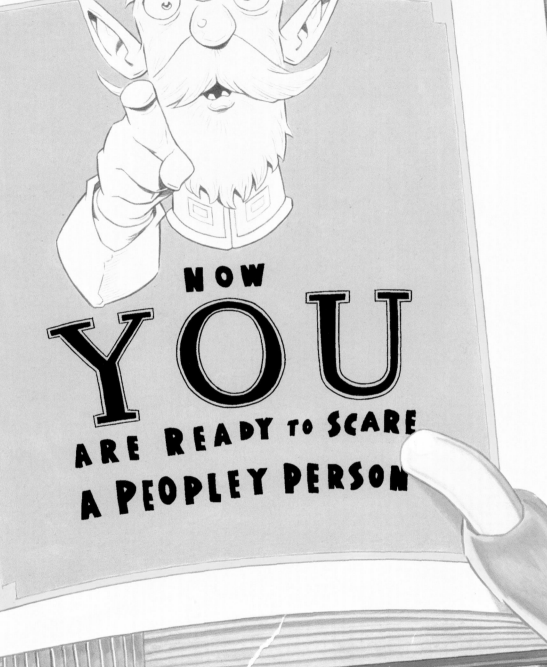

Of course, first of all Rufus would have to **FIND** a Peopley Person.

He cast his eyes over the desert.

All he saw was a van full of **vampires** and a **witch** on a motorbike.

There wasn't a single Peopley Person

ANYWHERE!

Rufus needed a change of plan.
Perhaps, he thought, he would find some
Peopley Persons in the big leafy forest.

But he was wrong.

All he saw was four **ghosts** and a **ghost dog**
on a family day out.

There wasn't a single Peopley Person

ANYWHERE!

That afternoon, Rufus decided to explore the
seven seas. He searched above AND below the waves.

Still, he had no luck.

All he saw was a **skeleton** in a speedboat, a **robot** on
a surfboard and some **mummies** in a submarine.

There wasn't a single Peopley Person
ANYWHERE!

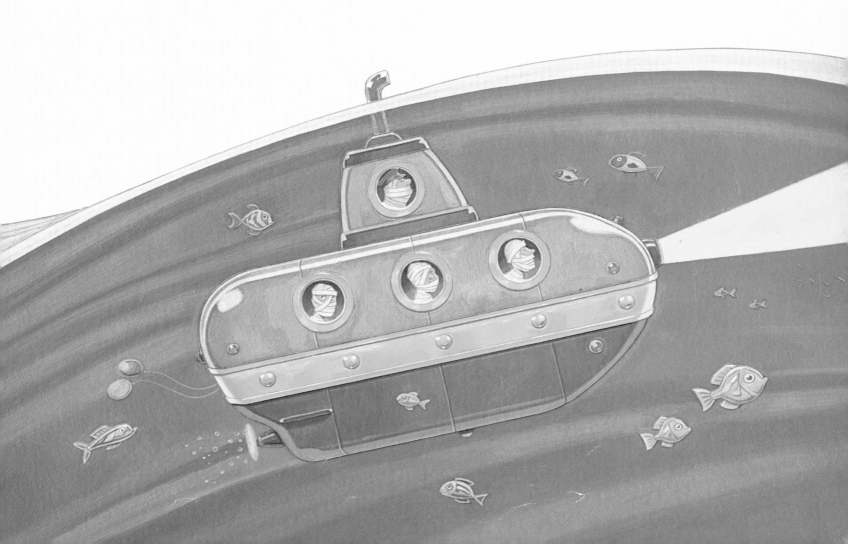

Poor old Rufus was down in the dumps,
but he wouldn't give up. Maybe there were
Peopley Persons in the clouds?

Once again, he was disappointed.

All he saw was a **werewolf** with a jetpack,
a **goblin** in a helicopter, a **ghoul** in a hang-glider,
a **troll** in a plane and an **alien** in a rocket.

There wasn't a single Peopley Person

ANYWHERE!

SUPER SPOOKY FANCY DRESS PARTY Saturday 7—
—THE BARN—

And so the search continued.
Once or twice, Rufus was certain
he'd found a Peopley Person . . .

. . . but he was wrong.

Soon, Rufus could hardly keep his eyes open.
He began to wonder if Peopley Persons
existed **AT ALL!**

Rufus was running out of places to look.
His legs were **wobbly**, his feet **ached** AND he'd run out
of **baked beans**. Everything seemed **HOPELESS!**

But just then, he heard a noise . . .

It was **music!** And it was coming from a barn.
The lights were on and it was full of laughter and **FUN!**

Rufus thought hard. He didn't know **ANY** creatures
that liked to have fun apart from . . .

PEOPLEY PERSONS!

AT LAST! HE'D FOUND SOME!

And so, **roaring** and **raging** and **ranting**,
he leapt towards the barn. Soon he'd be a

TIP-TOP SCARY MONSTER!

SUPER SPOOKY PARTY

But when Rufus got inside, he was
more disappointed than ever. All he saw was
a **super spooky party** in full swing.

There wasn't a single Peopley Person
ANYWHERE!

With a heavy heart, Rufus turned to leave,
but before he could go, a little ghost grabbed his hand.

"Don't be shy," it said, pulling him into the party.
"Come and have some **FUN!**"

Rufus was nervous.
He didn't really know **how** to have fun.

Luckily the little ghost was a **brilliant** teacher.

Together they danced . . .

. . . and they played.

They ate . . .   (maybe a bit too much)

. . . and then they laughed and laughed and **LAUGHED!**

Soon Rufus was having the time of his life!
When the party was over, they were exhausted.

The little ghost held her arms out wide.
"I'm Daisy," she said, "and I'm your friend **FOREVER!**"
Then Daisy did something **ASTOUNDING.**

Daisy wasn't a ghost at all!
She was a

PEOPLEY
PERSON!

RUFUS COULDN'T BELIEVE IT!

FINALLY!

This was his big
chance to become a
TIP-TOP SCARY MONSTER.

Rufus knew **EXACTLY**
what to do.

With his heart pounding,
he **LUNGED**
towards Daisy . . .

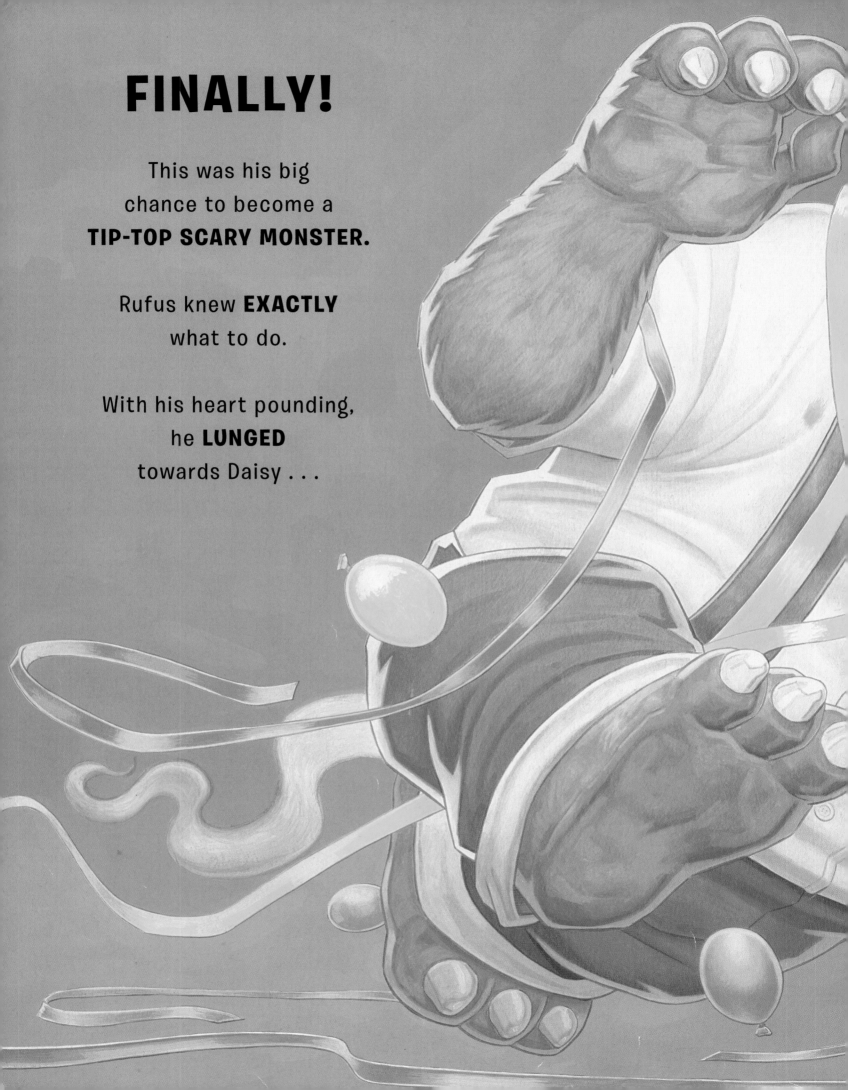

. . . and gave her a

MONSTER HUG!

"I'm Rufus," he smiled, "and I'm your **friend forever** too."

From that day onwards, Rufus and Daisy were never apart and, although Rufus may not have been a
TIP-TOP SCARY MONSTER . . .

. . . he was certainly a

HAPPY MONSTER!

For my own little monster, Alfie - S.B.

A TEMPLAR BOOK

First published in the UK in 2018 by Templar Publishing,
an imprint of Kings Road Publishing, part of the Bonnier Publishing Group,
The Plaza, 535 King's Road, London, SW10 0SZ
www.bonnierpublishing.com

1 3 5 7 9 10 8 6 4 2

ISBN 978-1-78741-008-4 (hardback)
978-1-78370-140-7 (paperback)

This book was typeset in Burbank Big Regular
The illustrations were painted in acrylic

Designed by Helen Chapman and Olivia Cook
Edited by Katie Haworth

Printed in Malaysia